P9-CQE-412

For Louis

SIMON & SCHUSTER BOOKS FOR YOUNG READERS
An imprint of Simon & Schuster Children's Publishing Division
1230 Avenue of the Americas, New York, New York 10020
Copyright © 2011 by Jeff Newman
All rights reserved, including the right of reproduction in whole or in part in any form.
SIMON & SCHUSTER BOOKS FOR YOUNG READERS is a trademark of Simon & Schuster, Inc.
For information about special discounts for bulk purchases, please contact Simon & Schuster
Special Sales at 1-866-506-1949 or business@simonandschuster.com.
The Simon & Schuster Speakers Bureau can bring authors to your live event.
For more information or to book an event, contact the Simon & Schuster Speakers Bureau
at 1-866-248-3049 or visit our website at www.simonspeakers.com.
Book design by Lizzy Bromley
The text for this book is set in Gill Sans.
The illustrations for this book are rendered in ink, permanent marker,
and gouache, and are digitally composited.
Manufactured in China
0611 SCP
10 9 8 7 6 5 4 3 2 1
Library of Congress Cataloging-in-Publication Data
Newman, Jeff, 1976–
Hand book / Jeff Newman. — 1st ed.
p. cm.
Summary: Follows a person's journey through life focusing on the hands and what they do,
from babyhood to adulthood, when a new pair of hands comes into existence.
ISBN 978-1-4169-5013-4 (hardcover : alk. paper)
[1. Stories in rhyme. 2. Hand—Fiction. 3. Growth—Fiction.] I. Title.
PZ8.3.N4649Han 2011
[E]—dc22
2010007017

first edition

HAND BOOK

Jeff Newman

Simon & Schuster
Books for Young Readers
New York   London   Toronto   Sydney

One hand.

Two hands.

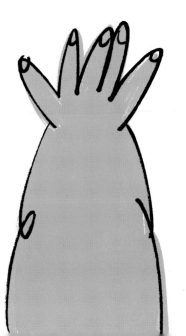

Two hands clap.

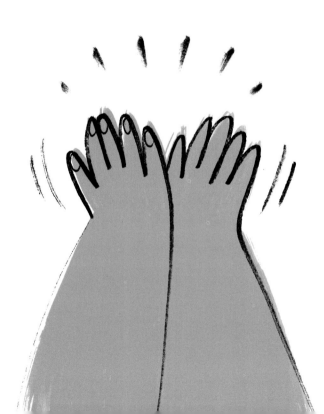

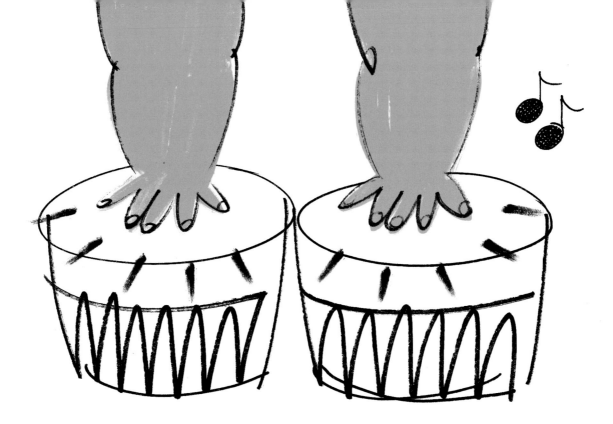

Two hands slap.

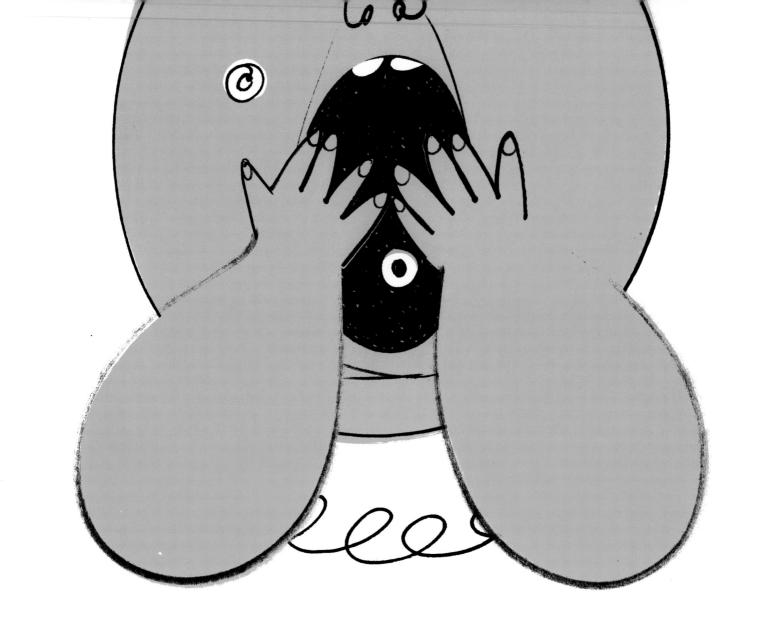

Hands to eat.

Hands (and feet).

Hands grip.

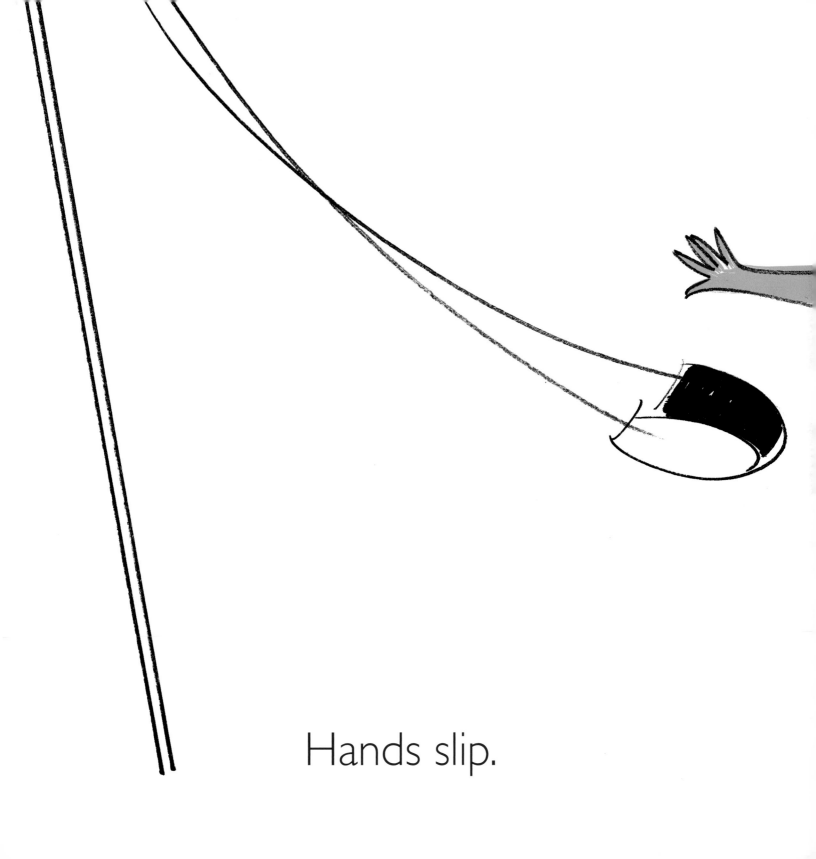

Hands slip.

Hands wash.

Hands dry.

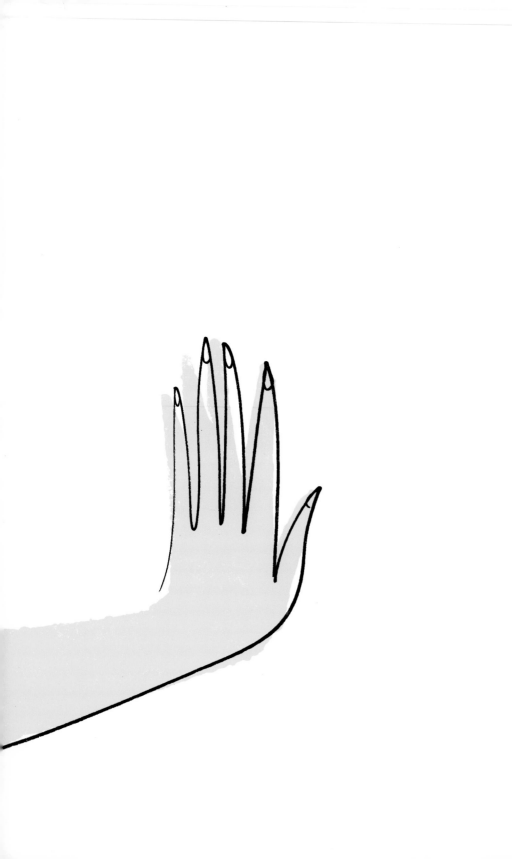

Hands say good-bye.

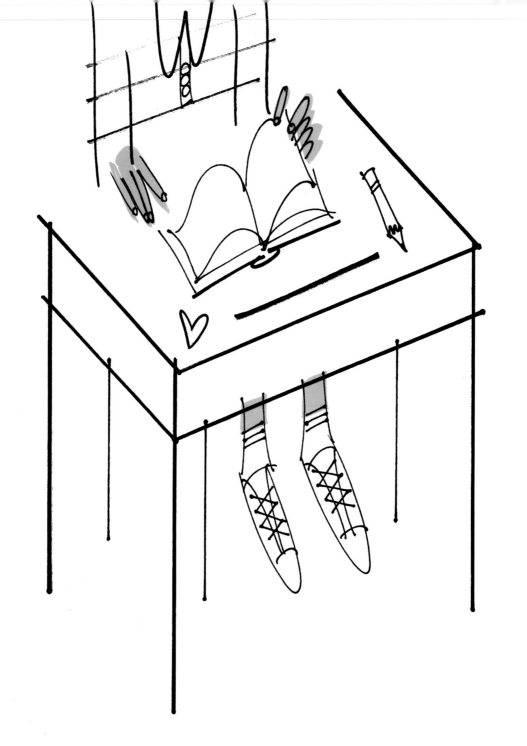

Hands turn.

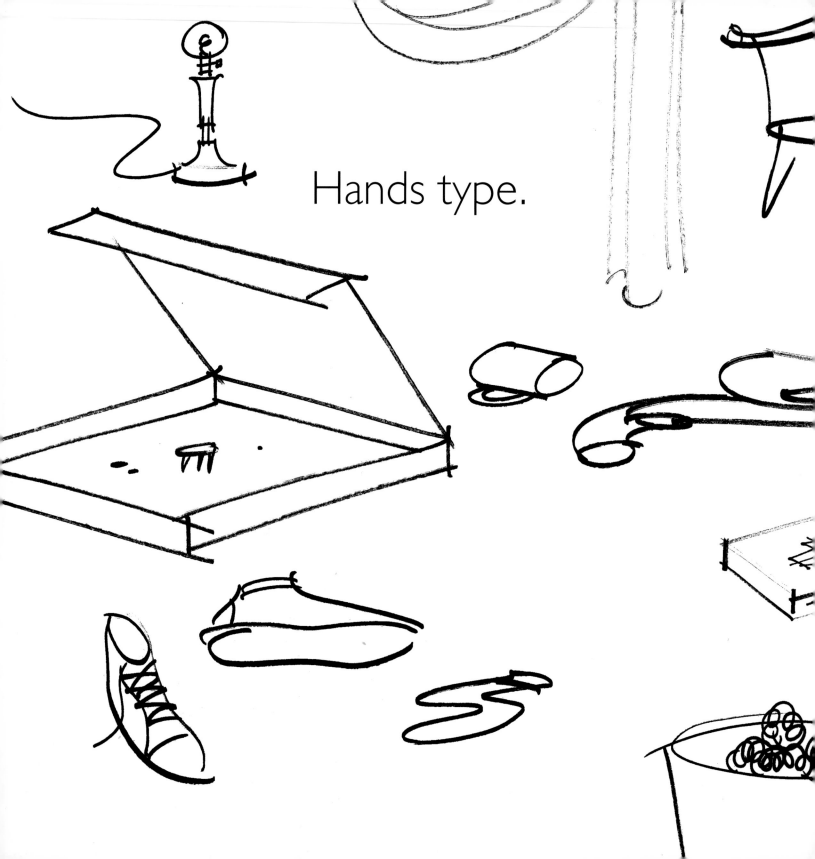

Hands type.

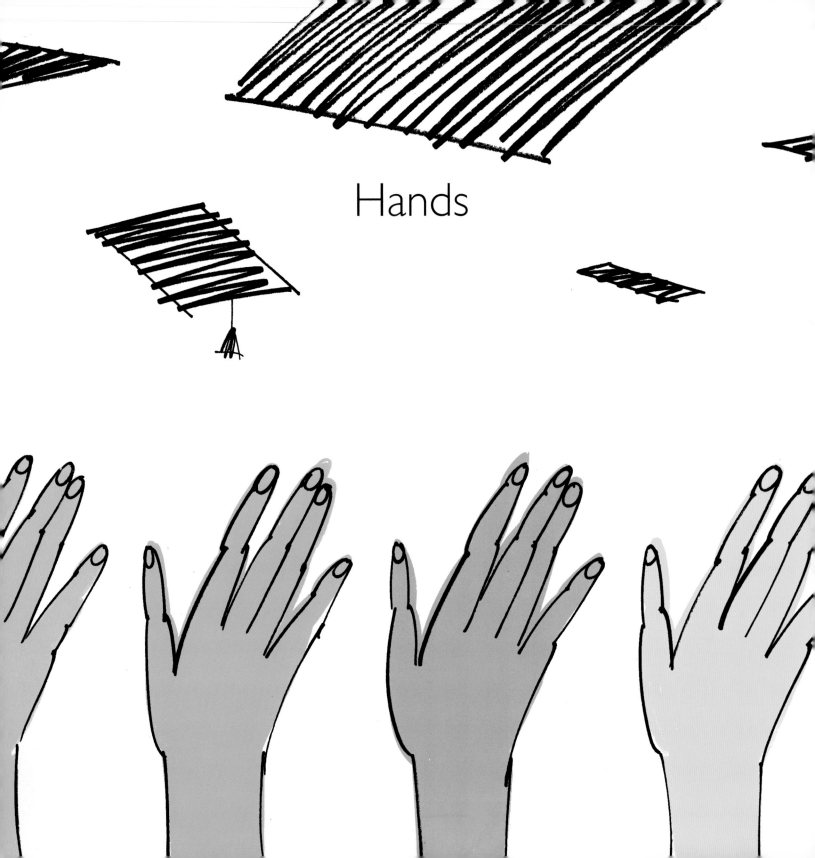

Hands

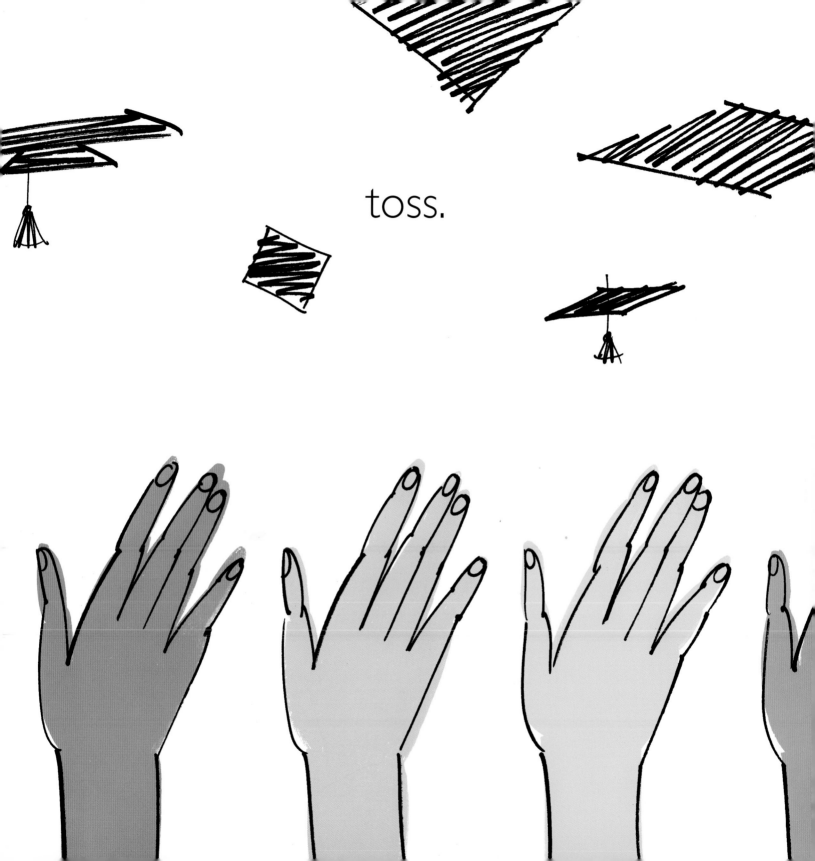

toss.

Hands cross.

Hands make.

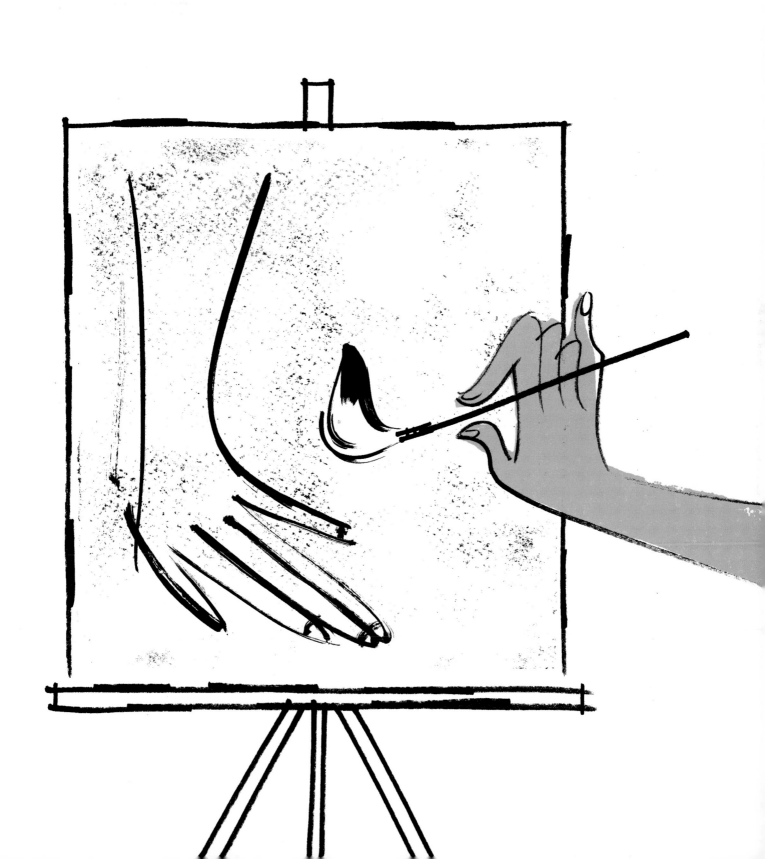

Hands shake

and hold

and then,

again,

one hand,

two hands,

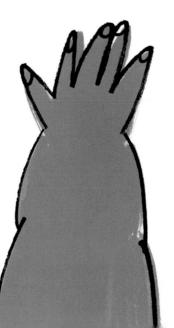

clap.

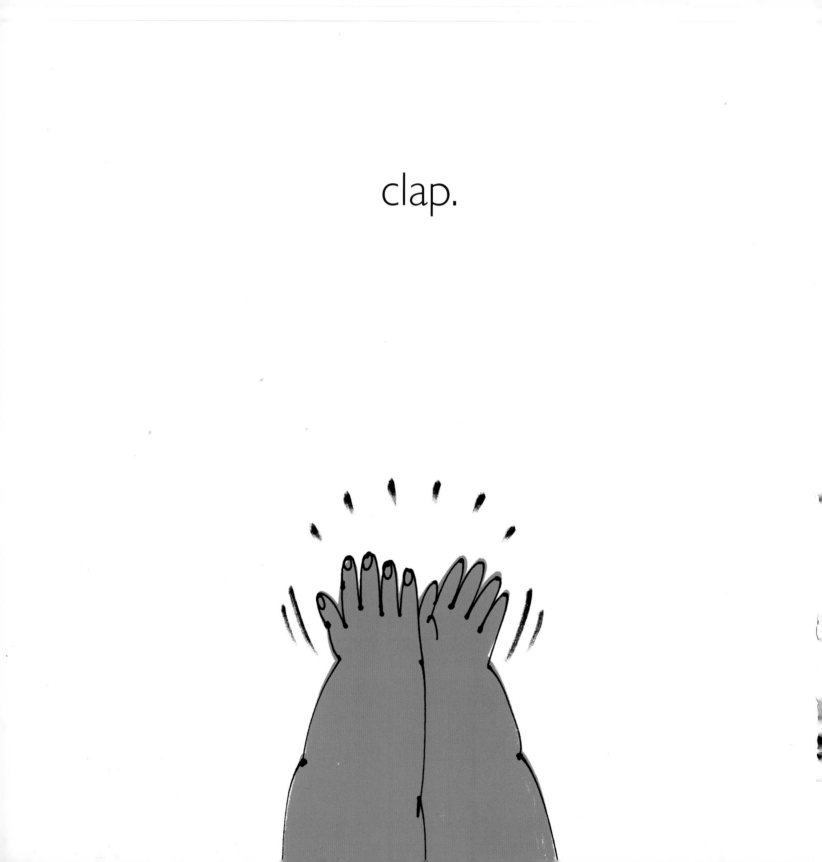

DISCARDED

J PICTURE NEWMAN
Newman, Jeff
Hand book

R0119175944   PTREE

PEACHTREE

Atlanta-Fulton Public Library